JOHNNY APPLESEED

JOHNNY

ROSEMARY AND STEPHEN VINCENT BENÉT

APPLESEED

ILLUSTRATED BY S. D. SCHINDLER WITH A NOTE FROM THOMAS C. BENÉT

Margaret K. McElderry Books
New York • London • Toronto • Sydney • Singapore

Margaret K. McElderry Books
An imprint of Simon & Schuster Children's Publishing Division
1230 Avenue of the Americas
New York, New York 10020

Book design by Dave Caplan and Jim Hoover
The text of this book is set in Celestia Antiqua.
The illustrations are rendered in colored pencil.

Printed in Hong Kong
10 9 8 7 6 5 4 3 2 1

Library of Congress Cataloging-in-Publication Data
Benét, Rosemary, 1900-
Johnny Appleseed / Rosemary and Stephen Vincent Benét ; illustrated by S. D. Schindler ; with a note from Thomas C. Benét. p. cm.
Summary: A poem describing Johnny Appleseed's appearance and actions.
1. Appleseed, Johnny, 1774-1845--Juvenile poetry. 2. Frontier and pioneer life--United States--Juvenile poetry. 3. Apple growers--United States--Juvenile poetry. 4. Children's poetry, American. [1. Appleseed, Johnny, 1774-1845--Poetry. 2. Frontier and pioneer life--Poetry. 3. American poetry.] I. Benét, Stephen Vincent, 1898-1943. II. Schindler, S. D., ill. III. Title.

PS3503.E53 J64 2001 811'.52--dc21 99-89391

ISBN 0-689-82975-2

Thanks to Emma, Ann, and Jim

—S. D. S.

f Jonathan Chapman
Two things are known
That he loved apples,
That he walked alone.

At seventy-odd
He was gnarled as could be,
But ruddy and sound
As a good apple tree.

For fifty years over
Of harvest and dew,
He planted his apples
Where no apples grew.

The winds of the prairie
Might blow through his rags,

But he carried his seeds
In the best deerskin bags.

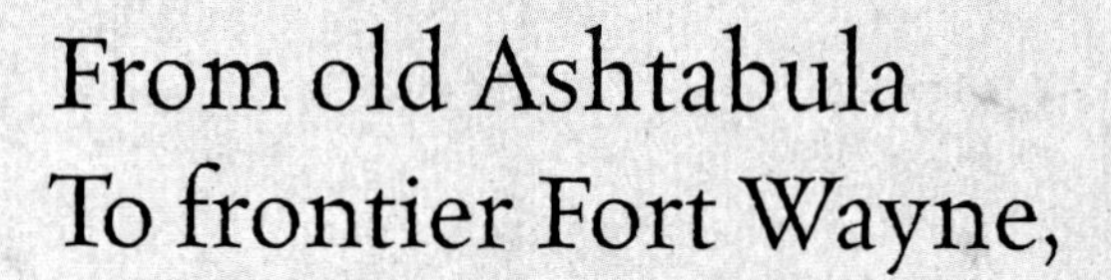

From old Ashtabula
To frontier Fort Wayne,

He planted and pruned
And he planted again.

Ashtabula
Fort Wayne
OHIO
INDIANA

He had not a hat
To encumber his head.
He wore a tin pan
On his white hair instead.

He nested with owl,
And with bear cub and 'possum,

And knew all his orchards
Root, tendril, and blossom.

A fine old man,
As ripe as a pippin,

His heart still light,
And his step still skipping.

The stalking Indian,
The beast in its lair
Did no hurt
While he was there.

For they could tell,
As wild things can,
That Jonathan Chapman
Was God's own man.

Why did he do it?
We do not know.
He wished that apples
Might root and grow.

He has no statue.
He has no tomb.
He has his apple trees
Still in bloom.

Consider, consider,
Think well upon
The marvelous story
Of Appleseed John.

My parents wrote the poem "Johnny Appleseed" for *A Book of Americans* during the summer of 1933, when I was seven years old. All of the poems in the book are about familiar American figures and events and were meant not only to inform, but also to entertain. I can remember the obvious pleasure my parents took in collaborating on *A Book of Americans*. They were a spirited couple who loved words and loved delving into this country's history and into the accomplishments and foibles of its famous personalities. Their goal was to capture in verse the spirit of a period in our history or of a person.

John Chapman was one such person. The picture that history gives us of John Chapman is touched with elements of folk legend, but he was a real man who did indeed wear a tin pan for a hat and garments some said were made out of coffee sacking. He planted apple seeds throughout the wilderness in what is now the Midwestern United States and would travel hundreds of miles to tend his orchards. The stories about him emphasize his kindness to animals and hold that Native Americans considered him a powerful medicine man. John Chapman—Johnny Appleseed—was a pioneer spirit, with a garland of apple blossoms.

The reference in the poem to the "stalking Indian" as a "wild thing" may seem to be a bit dated and to carry overtones of a less-enlightened period in history. The Indian in the poem was not stalking a person but was probably just stalking game, and the reference was used by my parents as an atmospheric touch. Actually, my parents were quite liberal for their time, as another poem in the volume attests:

But, just remember this about
Our ancestors so dear:
They didn't find an empty land.
The Indians were here.

—Thomas C. Benét
San Francisco